Everything You Need to Know About
the Stars of

HIGH SCHOOL MUSICAL 3

Zac &
Vanessa

Ashley

Corbin

By Jackie Robb

New York   Toronto   London   Auckland   Sydney
Mexico City   New Delhi   Hong Kong   Buenos Aires

Photo Copyright Credits

Front Cover: Zac Efron and Vanessa Hudgens: Jason Merritt/FilmMagic/Getty Images; Ashley Tisdale: Jon Kopaloff/FilmMagic/Getty Images; Corbin Bleu: Sara De Boer/Retna Ltd.
Back cover: Zac Efron: Michael Buckner/2008 Getty Images; Vanessa Anne Hudgens: Adam Orchon/Everett Collection; Ashley Tisdale and Corbin Bleu: PNP/ WENN/Newscom.

Page 1: Zac Efron and Vanessa Hudgens: Jason Merritt/FilmMagic/Getty Images; Ashley Tisdale: Jon Kopaloff/FilmMagic/Getty Images; Corbin Bleu: Sara De Boer/Retna Ltd. **Page 3:** infphoto/Newscom. **Page 4:** (Top) Noel Vasquez/Getty Images; (bottom, left to right) Byron Purvis/AdMedia/Sipa Press; Adam Orchon/Everett Collection. **Page 5:** (Top to bottom) allstarphotos/Newscom; Dee Cercone/Everett Collection; Giulio Marcocchi/Sipa Press/Newscom; Mark Savage/Corbis. **Page 6:** (Top to bottom) allstarphotos/Newscom; Jesse Grant/WireImage/Getty Images; Marcel Thomas/FilmMagic/Getty Images; Janet Macoska/Retna Ltd. **Page 7:** (Top) Noel Vasquez/Getty Images; (bottom, left to right) W6005Y/AAD/starmax/Newscom; Mark Sullivan/WireImage/Getty Images. **Page 8:** (Top to bottom, left column) allstarphotos/Newscom; Tony Gonzalez/Everett Collection; Dee Cercone/Everett Collection; Axel Koester/Corbis; (right) Lionel Hahn/ABACAUSA/Newscom. **Page 9:** (Top to bottom): Mark Savage/Corbis; Adam Orchon/Everett Collection; Michael Buckner/Getty Images; Tammie Arroyo/AP Photo. **Page 10:** (Top to bottom): Dee Cercone/Everett Collection; Noel Vasquez/Getty Images; Adam Orchon/Everett Collection; Kevin Winter/Getty Images. **Page 11:** (On left) Seth Browarnik/WireImage/Getty Images; (top to bottom, right column) Noel Vasquez/Getty Images; Scott Gries/Getty Images; Alexandra Wyman/WireImage/Getty Images; Adam Orchon/Everett Collection. **Page 12:** (Top to bottom) Theo Wargo/WireImage/Getty Images; Jesse Grant/Getty Images/Newscom; Scott Gries/Getty Images; Marcel Thomas/FilmMagic/Getty Images. **Page 13:** Gregg DeGuire/WireImage/Getty Images. **Page 14:** (Top to bottom) Jeffrey Mayer/WireImage/Getty Images; Jesse Grant/WireImage/Getty Images; INF Photos agency/Newscom; INF Photos agency/Newscom. **Page 15:** Dee Cercone/Everett Collection. **Page 16:** Lionel Hahn/ABACAUSA/Newscom. **Page 17:** (Top to bottom) Sara De Boer/Retna Ltd.; Sara De Boer/Retna Ltd.; Michael Tran/FilmMagic/Getty Images; Gary Lewis/PA Photos/Retna Ltd. **Page 18:** (Top to bottom) Frederick M. Brown/Getty Images; Dan MacMedan/WireImage/Getty Images; Kevin Mazur/Getty Images; Jeff Kravitz/FilmMagic/Newscom. **Page 19:** Adam Orchon/Everett Collection. **Page 20:** (Top to bottom) Sara De Boer/Retna Ltd.; Adam Orchon/Everett Collection; Sara De Boer/Retna Ltd.; INF Photos agency/Newscom. **Page 21:** Sara De Boer/Retna Ltd. **Page 22:** (Top to bottom) Alexander Tamargo/Getty Images; John Parra/WireImage/Getty Images; Theo Wargo/WireImage/Getty Images; allstarphotos/Newscom. **Page 23:** EMPICS Entertainment/Retna Ltd. **Page 24:** (Top to bottom) Sara De Boer/Retna Ltd.; Adam Orchon/Everett Collection; Jason Merritt/FilmMagic/Getty Images; RD/Leon/Retna Digital. **Page 25:** David Atlas/Retna Ltd. **Page 26:** (Top to bottom) Scott Gries/Getty Images; Walter McBride/Retna Ltd.; Scott Gries/Getty Images; Theo Wargo/WireImage/Getty Images. **Page 27:** Dee Cercone/Everett Collection. **Page 28:** (Top to bottom) allstarphotos/Newscom; Jordan Strauss/WireImage/Getty Images; Scott Gries/Getty Images; Steve Granitz/Getty Images. **Page 29:** Michael Buckner/Getty Images. **Page 30:** (Top to bottom) Michael Loccisano/FilmMagic/Getty Images; Marcel Thomas/FilmMagic/Getty Images; Michael Buckner/Getty Images; Kevin Winter/Getty Images. **Page 31:** Jon Kopaloff/FilmMagic/Getty Images. **Page 32:** (Top to bottom) Bob Riha, Jr./WireImage/Getty Images; Maury Phillips/WireImage/Getty Images; Michael Bezjian/WireImage/Getty Images; allstarphotos/Newscom. **Page 33:** Ciao Hollywood/Splash News/Newscom. **Page 34:** (Top to bottom) Ciao Hollywood/Splash News/Newscom; allstarphotos/Newscom; Dennis Van Tine/Abaca Press/MCT/Newscom; Lane Ericcson-PHOTOlink/Newscom. **Page 35:** zumalive/Newscom. **Page 36:** (Top to bottom) Sara De Boer/Retna Ltd.; Byron Purvis/AdMedia/Sipa Press; allstarphotos/Newscom; Isabella/Prahl/Splash News/Newscom. **Page 37:** Kathy Hutchins/Hutchins Photo/Showcase/Newscom. **Page 38:** (Top to bottom) Michael Tran/FilmMagic/Getty Images; Axel/ZUMA Press; Don Arnold/WireImage/Getty Images; Frazer Harrison/Getty Images. **Page 39:** Dee Cercone/Everett Collection. **Page 40:** (Top to bottom, left column) David Livingston/Getty Images; Kane Hibberd/Getty Images; uniphotos/Newscom; Jordan Strauss/Getty Images; (right) Gaye Gerard/Getty Images. **Page 41:** Ash Knotek/Snappers/ZUMA Press. **Page 42:** (Top to bottom) Paul Fenton/ZUMA Press; Baxter/ABACAUSA/Newscom; Kathy Hutchins/Hutchins Photo/Showcase/Newscom; Dee Cercone/Everett Collection. **Page 43:** Dee Cercone/Everett Collection. **Page 44:** (Top to bottom) Splash News/Newscom; Ash Knotek/Snappers/ZUMA Press; Splash News/Newscom; Marsaili McGrath/Getty Images for Idesigns Event Services/Newscom. **Page 45:** (Top to bottom) Gregg DeGuire/WireImage/Getty Images; Adam Orchon/Everett Collection; Kevin Mazur/WireImage/Getty Images. **Page 46:** (Top to bottom) Jon Kopaloff/FilmMagic/Getty Images; Kathy Hutchins/Hutchins Photo/Showcase/Newscom; Ash Knotek/Snappers/ZUMA Press. **Page 47:** (Top to bottom) Dee Cercone/Everett Collection; allstarphotos/Newscom; Dee Cercone/Everett Collection. **Page 48:** (Top to bottom) Janet Macoska/Retna Ltd.; Michael Tran/FilmMagic/Getty Images; Paul Fenton/ZUMA Press.

ISBN-10: 0-545-08570-5
ISBN-13: 978-0-545-08570-0

© 2008 Scholastic Inc.

Published by Scholastic Inc.
SCHOLASTIC and associated logos are trademarks and/or registered trademarks of Scholastic Inc.

12 11 10 9 8 7 6 5 4 3 2   8 9 10/0

Designed by Jenn Martino
Printed in the U.S.A.
First printing, September 2008

INTRODUCTION

Fans of *High School Musical* were singing and dancing in the aisles when they heard the news — not only was the Disney Channel planning a "three-quel" of the amazingly successful movies, but it would be a big screen release, opening in theaters across the country on October 24, 2008. And there was even more to cheer about — all of the movies' talented stars, Zac Efron, Vanessa Anne Hudgens, Ashley Tisdale, Corbin Bleu, Lucas Grabeel, and Monique Coleman are back at East High, playing the roles that made them household names and faces!

There's no doubt that *High School Musical* is here to stay, and it will always be number one in the hearts of its fans! But the buzz about *HSM3* is just beginning. Everyone wants to know: Will Troy and Gabriella stay together? Will Sharpay and Ryan steal the show? Will Chad and Taylor keep on dancin'?

In the following pages, you'll learn tons of new facts about the *HSM* gang. So put on your dancing shoes and get ready for the 411 about the stars of the film event of the year!

THEY'RE BACK... AND SO ARE WE!

The gang from East High are getting ready for a very special school year — their senior year. Troy, Gabbie, Sharpay, Ryan, Chad, and Taylor will be saying — and singing — good-bye to their high school in a big way, and on the big screen, when *High School Musical 3* hits theaters in October.

Director and choreographer Kenny Ortega, who's been manning the movie's dance moves from the very first step, was delighted to learn that the entire cast was returning for the third installment, but he hinted that it might be the last time this particular group of friends would be walking through the halls of East High. He told MTV, "I'm just the luckiest guy, and I know it. This will be our last time together, and I love working with these kids so much. It's great to be able to do this again for the fans."

THE STARS DISH ON *HSM3* . . .

"It's senior year, so there will be graduation and a prom,"

– Vanessa Hudgens

"I'm excited, but it's going to be sad, I think. It seems like it will really be like graduation, and I know I'll be crying like crazy when we're filming."

– Ashley Tisdale

"I am so excited to see Taylor deal with what college she wants to go to, and to go to prom. I'm so proud to be a part of *High School Musical*, and I really love my life. This is all so unbelievable, to know that the fans love the movie so much and want to see us again."

– Monique Coleman

"I wouldn't want to miss being a part of this. I'm glad to have the chance to have one last, big hurrah, and I promise the fans I'm going to give my all to this, to really be the best I can be for them."

– Corbin Bleu

SO WHAT EXACTLY IS *HIGH SCHOOL MUSICAL 3* GOING TO BE ABOUT?

Well, although the plot is a total secret, all the stars have let the basic storyline slip. "There will be problems for Gabriella and Troy, because they have to face the fact that they might be going to different colleges, and they have to deal with the possibility of losing one another," Vanessa informed People.com. But according to a Disney Channel spokesperson, the movie will definitely feature its trademark "let's put on a show" power ending as Gabriella, Troy, and the rest of the Wildcats stage a spring musical that completely reflects their experience at East High, and their hopes and fears for the future. "There will be plenty of music, plenty of laughs and tears, and plenty of drama — just like in a real high school," says Ashley.

THE *HIGH SCHOOL MUSICAL* PHENOMENON!

It came out of nowhere, a little movie musical that the Disney Channel thought might get a few fans tapping their toes and singing along. But when *High School Musical* made its debut on January 20, 2006, no one was prepared for the film's success, or the huge hold it would have over viewers who were ready to "get their heads in the game."

Zac Efron, who portrays jock-extraordinaire Troy, told *J-14* that the movie's positive message made it a fan favorite. "The message in the movie is you have to follow your own path," he explained. "Don't listen to all the pressures in the outside world. Troy starts off as a hotshot, but he's given that name by his peers — that's not who he is." Vanessa Anne Hudgens, who plays smart gal Gab, agrees, and adds, "The message of the movie is to conquer your fears. Troy and Gabriella start as the jock and the genius girl — music brings them and the whole school together."

The film aired on the Disney Channel on January 20, 2006 — and it wasn't long before the producers knew they had a hit on their hands. *HSM* was the highest-rated original TV movie on any cable channel — 7.7 million viewers had been glued to their TV sets that night. By the time the Disney Channel had aired the movie on seven nights between January and February, over 28.3 million fans had watched — and watched again.

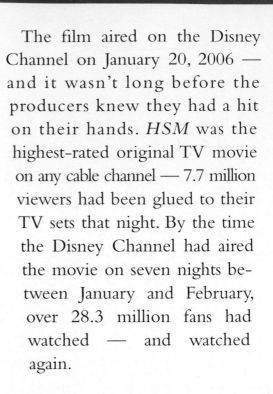

But fans weren't just watching, they were listening. The *HSM* soundtrack album became the No. 1 selling CD on iTunes, and the No. 1 selling CD on Amazon.com. And by February 2006, the soundtrack had hit the No. 1 spot on *Billboard*'s Top 200 Albums Chart, and nine singles from the album were on the *Billboard* Pop Singles Chart. When the DVD became available in May of 2006, it became a huge bestseller, and fans were thrilled with the DVD's fun extras, like Kenny Ortega's dance lessons and the behind-the-scenes peeks at the making of the musical.

It was a no-brainer that Disney would want to make a sequel to *HSM*.

And even before the fans saw one scene from *HSM2*, the film's first single, "What Time Is It?", became a hit on the pop charts. Director Kenny Ortega told People.com that he knew the opening scene of *HSM2* would be the place where he re-introduced all the characters, and he wanted a fun song to help bring the audience back to school. "We wanted a song about how it feels to start your first day of summer, and to establish what each of them have in mind for the next few months."

Monique Coleman, who plays the bouncy Taylor, told People.com that the sequel's story was, " . . . more emotional, deeper, and more sensitive. It's about honoring those decisions that you make, and recognizing that when you don't make the right decisions, you have the right to change your mind. The songs have a real '50s feel, very awesome music — some of the songs feel very old-fashioned, and there's real romance to them. I think the whole movie just has a very deep feeling to it."

Corbin Bleu, the basketball hotshot Chad, was excited to see that his character and Taylor were starting to explore a possible romance, too. "My character and Taylor, we sort of have a little spark going on," he told *J-14*. "That continues through the second movie. We like each other, but we sort of keep a distance from each other. It's a cute relationship."

And even Sharpay had a chance at love in *HSM2*, when Zeke — a basketball star with a warm spot in his heart for cooking and baking, played by Chris Warren — pursued his crush on her.

HSM2 FAST FAX

- HSM2 DEBUTED ON THE DISNEY CHANNEL ON AUGUST 17, 2007.
- THE MOVIE'S PREMIERE WAS WATCHED BY 17.2 MILLION VIEWERS.
- IT WAS THE HIGHEST-RATED BASIC CABLE BROADCAST IN U.S. HISTORY!
- MORE THAN 88 MILLION PEOPLE WORLDWIDE HAVE SEEN HSM2.
- THE HSM2 SOUNDTRACK REACHED NO. 1 ON THE BILLBOARD CHART.

WHAT'S THE SECRET BEHIND THE *HSM* PHENOMENON?

"I think there's something about this story that touches everyone, whether you're in high school now, whether you're going into high school, or whether you ever were in high school. The story holds you, and it has meaning for you, because you know these people — you see them in your own school. You might even be Troy or Chad or Gabriella or Taylor, and you see these characters succeed, and you know you can, too."
- CORBIN BLEU

"This is a story that tells you how important it is to be true to yourself, and to never let other people hold you back. Once you see this movie, I think you want to go out and conquer the world."
- ASHLEY TISDALE

ZAC EFRON: THE JOY OF TROY

When Zac Efron was a student in high school, he was definitely not a boy like Troy Bolton. "I wasn't the coolest kid in school," he told *Newsday*. "I wasn't good at sports, and I was really small when I was younger. I was pretty bad at Little League, and I hate to admit this, but I think I scored two points my entire basketball season."

FAST FAX

BIRTH DATE: OCTOBER 18, 1987

BIRTH NAME: ZACHARY DAVID ALEXANDER EFRON

HOMETOWN: SAN LUIS OBISPO, CA

IN THE BEGINNING . . .

Zac has always had a passion for performing. Before he celebrated his 13th birthday, Zac was appearing in school and community theater productions, receiving rave reviews from his classmates and family friends when he appeared in musicals like *Gypsy*, *Peter Pan*, and *The Music Man*. By the time he was in 9th grade, Zac was already a professional actor, catching the attention of casting agents and directors in Los Angeles. With his dazzling smile and bright personality, he had no trouble winning roles, and soon he was appearing in TV shows like *Summerland*, *ER*, and *Firefly*.

THE HSM EXPERIENCE

When Zac auditioned for the part of Troy in *High School Musical*, he had a feeling this role would be a special one. He was happy to share his own love of musicals with a new, young audience. "I grew up watching *Grease*," he told People.com. "I used to love that movie, and all the Disney animated movies. Music was a part of films. That's what made me excited, that we brought that back a little bit . . ."

HAIRSPRAY

Zac's first big-screen movie following *HSM* was another high-energy movie musical: *Hairspray*. The movie was a whole new ballgame for Zac. The cast was filled with huge stars like John Travolta and Michelle Pfeiffer. "I was stoked to get the role," he told *USA Today*. "I saw *Hairspray* on Broadway, and that was very cool. I never imagined I would be a part of the movie, but I was really lucky to be selected."

The movie was released on July 27, 2007, to rave reviews. Zac's portrayal of Link Larkin was a sweet success, and not only did he bring all his *HSM* fans along for the ride, he also found a slew of new fans. Zac himself couldn't stop gushing over the film, " . . . the whole thing was amazing, like a dream in real life."

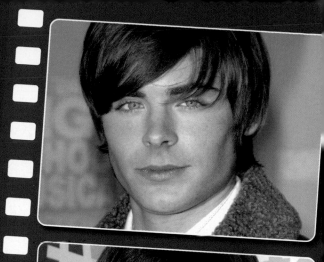

TO PORTRAY THE HEARTTHROBBY LINK LARKIN, ZAC DYED HIS HAIR BLACK AND GAINED ABOUT 15 POUNDS.

HSM . . . ROUND TWO!

The second he finished filming *Hairspray*, Zac flew back to Utah where *High School Musical 2* was in production. Delighted to be back in the role of Troy, Zac jumped into action and found things were just as much fun back at East High. "There's something amazing about working with these people, they're just the best," Zac said of his castmates during a *USA Today* interview. "When I got back to Utah and saw them all, it was like I took a deep breath and relaxed. We're all so close now. Everyone was really enthusiastic again, and we felt excited the whole time, so glad to be a part of it."

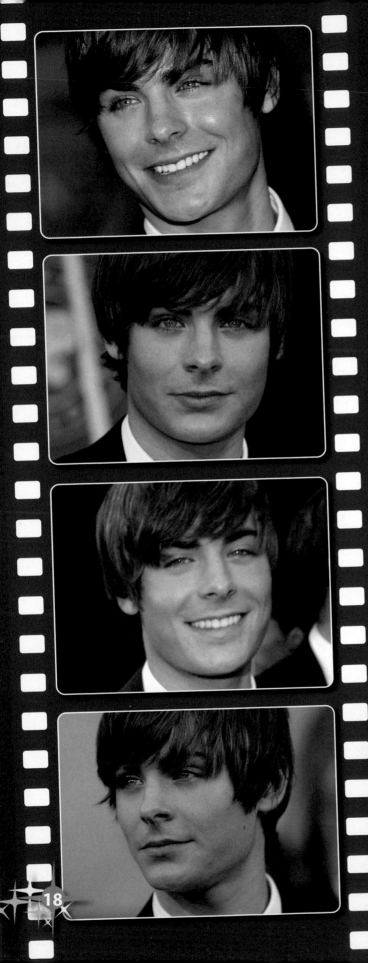

THE FINAL INSTALLMENT

While back in Utah filming the third *HSM* film, Zac admitted to feeling torn about the possibility of it being the last time he steps into the East High halls and puts on a Wildcats uniform. "I know I'll be sad to see us split up, because we really became a part of one big family. And I think we made good movies with good messages for everyone, messages about staying true to yourself and being positive, working together and being loyal to your friends, working hard to achieve your goals. All those elements were in the story, and I think that's what made the story so appealing. And yeah, it's going to be hard to say good-bye. But I think we're all ready to try new things and find our way. I hope our fans will stick with us through it all, to see where we all wind up!"

VANESSA ANNE HUDGENS: LEADING LADY!

Bright, beautiful, energetic, and completely talented, Vanessa Anne Hudgens has always had her eyes on the bright lights of Hollywood. But she never imagined she would become a part of the biggest movie musical success of them all.

FAST FAX
BIRTH DATE: DECEMBER 14, 1988
BIRTH NAME: VANESSA ANNE HUDGENS
HOMETOWN: SALINAS, CA

STARTING OUT . . .

When Vanessa was a young girl, she loved performing. She would bounce about the house belting out songs for her parents. She began to take dancing and singing lessons — and soon after she was auditioning for (and winning) parts in local community theater productions. Then one day, a friend from one of the local theaters asked Vanessa if she could do her a favor: She had an audition for a commercial and couldn't make it . . . would Vanessa go in her place? Vanessa went, and she did such a great job that she was hired immediately.

THE BIG SCREEN

Vanessa's career began taking off, and her family decided to move to Los Angeles so she could pursue her acting dreams. She took small roles on TV shows when one day, her mom took her to audition for a film called *Thirteen*. She got the part and won rave reviews. Her second movie, *Thunderbirds*, was an adventure film, and this time Vanessa had the leading role of Tintin. The movie was an action-adventure, science-fiction extravaganza, and Vanessa was thrilled. "I loved it," she told *San Diego Magazine*. "It's full of action. It got my adrenaline pumping every minute."

HSM HYSTERIA

But none of Vanessa's previous experiences could have possibly prepared her for the colossal success of *High School Musical* and *HSM2*, films that would give her the chance to show off all of her talents and introduced her to a massive audience around the world. "You couldn't have expected anything like that!" she gushed to *USA Today*. "I never imagined this would happen this way. It just was the biggest surprise in the world."

FILM FRIENDSHIPS

Vanessa made valuable friendships on-set with her *HSM* costars Ashley Tisdale and Monique Coleman. "Ashley is my best friend," she told *J-14*. "We understand each other, and we can talk about anything. And Monique is someone else I can talk to. I love gabbing with my girlfriends, shopping and giggling and having fun. I couldn't believe it — because sometimes you go to work on a set, and you meet people and you don't always get along so well. So it's a real pleasure to get the chance to meet people and become friends — and best friends, close friends!"

AND MORE!

Although she doesn't talk about it publicly, most fans also know that Vanessa made another close friend on the set — in fact, she found romance! Her onscreen leading man, Zac Efron, became her offscreen love as well, and they were soon seen vacationing in Hawaii and walking hand-in-hand at movie premieres. But when asked about her personal life, Vanessa usually says: "I don't like to talk about that."

V — THE ALBUM

Once fans got the chance to hear Vanessa's awesome voice, they begged for more. She was signed to Hollywood Records and recorded her debut solo CD, *V*. The success of the album gave her the opportunity to tour as an opening act for the Cheetah Girls — and she gave audiences a chance to hear her do what she had loved to do since she was a child: sing. "The stage always felt like my home," she told CosmoGirl.com. "That's where I grew up, doing musicals back at home. I get nervous before a show, but once I get on the stage, I literally calm down, feel at home, and just have fun. That's my calling."

ON *HSM3* . . .

Now, she's back at her other home away from home — the halls of East High. And she hopes that Gabriella will have an exciting senior year. "It's so awesome to think of her going to prom and graduating," she told People.com. "I can't wait to see what will happen between Gabriella and Troy. I think their love just might last forever."

ASHLEY TISDALE: DRAMA QUEEN

As a child, curly-haired Ashley Tisdale loved attention. Little Ashley was always singing and dancing and putting on shows for her family. And Ashley attracted attention from others as well. "I had this crazy, curly brown hair, really curly like Shirley Temple, when I was younger," she explained to *J-14*. "I guess people noticed me."

FAST FAX

BIRTH DATE: JULY 2, 1985
BIRTH NAME: ASHLEY MICHELLE TISDALE
HOMETOWN: WEST DEAL, NJ

A YOUNG STAR

One very important person who noticed Ashley was Bill Pearlman, a show-business manager. He saw her at a local mall, and noticed that she had a sparkle about her. He approached Ashley's mother, suggesting that perhaps Ashley might start auditioning for commercials and doing some modeling. Although her mom was initially hesitant, Ashley proved it was the right choice when she nabbed her first six commercial auditions. Ashley then began trying out for musicals and won the role of Cosette in *Les Misérables*. She also scored a role in *Annie*, in a touring company that traveled around the world.

THE SWEET LIFE

Ashley and her family decided to move to California to help her acting career bloom. Once there, she appeared on shows like *7th Heaven*, *Charmed*, and *Malcolm in the Middle*. But she was always searching for that one special role. She found it when Disney offered her the part of Maddie on *The Suite Life of Zack and Cody*. The show was a bona fide hit from the get-go, and Ashley was soon being recognized everywhere she went by devoted fans. "The fans saw me as Maddie, and that was OK because Maddie is much closer to me than anyone I've ever played," she told *J-14*. "The show was huge — I couldn't believe how many people watched."

THE NEXT BIG THING

It was while she was working on *Suite Life* that the producers of *HSM* caught sight of her, and thought she'd be perfect to play the diva dancing-queen Sharpay. Ashley was psyched to get the chance to play a nasty girl like Sharpay. "Oh yes, she rules the school," she told *J-14*. "She's the kind of girl that everyone knows though — unfortunately, I think there are a few Sharpays in every school. But even though a lot of people hate her, I can definitely relate to her passion for theater. I know what it feels like to want to be in musicals and to love being a part of life on the stage."

HEADSTRONG

On the *HSM* set, Ashley became close pals with Vanessa Anne Hudgens, and like Vanessa, Ashley parlayed her *HSM* success into a chance to record a solo CD called *Headstrong*. "I wanted to do an album for a long time," she told People.com. "Music has always been in my life, and it's always been a passion of mine along with acting. Vanessa and I both talked about it — we didn't want our albums to just be spin-offs from the movie, we wanted to make music that was our own and totally separate from *High School Musical*. I'd written songs before; I took voice lessons; and I was interested in pursuing music, too, but *High School Musical* definitely opened the door for me. It's given me the chance to do so many things, and I'm so glad about that."

ASHLEY ON *HSM3*

With *High School Musical 3*, Ashley hopes that Sharpay might have a chance to redeem herself — perhaps even be the star of the show again. But she knows that audiences will absolutely want to see Sharpay at her meanest. "Even though audiences hate Sharpay, they love to hate her," she explained to *J-14.* "It can't just be, 'Oh, we hate Sharpay!' You have to be entertained by her, and you have to want to see her in the movie. You have to think, 'Wow, I would miss her if she wasn't here!'" And what does Ashley think the future holds for Sharpay? "I think she'll always be a diva, and she'll always want to be the star of the show," she told People.com. "I don't think anyone would want her any other way!"

CORBIN BLEU'S READY TO DANCE!

When some performers say they've been dancing or singing since they were children, they might be exaggerating, but 19-year-old Corbin Bleu would be telling you the absolute truth. He's been tapping his toes since he was two!

FAST FAX
BIRTH DATE: FEBRUARY 21, 1989
BIRTH NAME: CORBIN BLEU REIVERS
HOMETOWN: BROOKLYN, NY

BABY BLEU

From the moment tiny Corbin could walk, he was dancing — and was he ever cute! Because Corbin was so adorable, he was quickly hired as a child model and appeared in many commercials. His parents eventually moved their family to Los Angles, and as Corbin grew, his desire to act grew with him. Having a dad who was already an actor gave Corbin a clear picture of what his career choice meant. In addition to his appearances in commercials, Corbin's parents encouraged him to take dance lessons. Although he was naturally graceful and a strong dancer, his classes helped him improve his skills, and soon he was performing in local community theater productions.

THE EARLY YEARS

By the late 1990s, Corbin was appearing in TV shows like *ER* and *Flight 29 Down,* and nabbing roles in movies like *Galaxy Quest* and *Catch That Kid.* Despite the fact that he was working all the time, Corbin also remained dedicated to living a "regular" life — his parents had helped him understand the importance of that. He attended the Los Angeles County School of Arts and the Debbie Allen Dance Academy, and he graduated from high school with honors. He also attended his proms, as well as other special school occasions, and kept closely connected with his high-school mates.

THE *HSM* EXPERIENCE

Perhaps it was that deep connection to his high-school experience that made Corbin such a natural for the role of Chad Danforth. His theater and dancing backgrounds made him a perfect fit for Chad, and although he'd never appeared in a musical before, he was ready for the challenge.

Another thing that was a challenge for Corbin? Basketball. "I have a hoop in my backyard, and I played when I was younger, but I don't exactly play, no," he told *J-14*. "We all actually went for two weeks of training, so we could get better, and some of the guys could play well, but I was, like, starting from scratch. By the end of the training, I could spin a basketball on my finger, but I was really struggling in the game in the beginning. I was always happy to go back to dancing, because dancing was something I could do."

ANOTHER SIDE OF CORBIN

Corbin's powerful singing voice led him to the recording studio, and in May 2007, Corbin released his debut CD, *Another Side*. The album was a huge success, and Corbin soon found himself touring both with the *HSM* cast and on his own in support of his CD. "My album . . . that was special," he told People.com. "The album gave me a chance to really show who I am to the world."

MORE MOVIES!

HSM2 brought Corbin back with his gang, and he was amazed again at how well they worked together and how close they were. While filming *HSM3*, Corbin was bursting with excitement over the fact that the gang would be back — this time on the big screen. "We are all so excited about this being in movie theaters," he told *J-14*. "That's so amazing for us. And to see everyone again, to be back together, that's just great. It's wonderful to work with such amazing people."

LUCAS GRABEEL'S THE GUY IN THE HAT!

From a young age, Lucas loved the spotlight, whether it was at home, at church where he played the drums in the band, in the men's *a cappella* singing groups he started, and even on the school's debate team. He definitely had that special something that spelled superstardom.

FAST FAX
BIRTH DATE: NOVEMBER 23, 1984
BIRTH NAME: LUCAS STEPHAN GRABEEL
HOMETOWN: SPRINGFIELD, MO

STARTING SMALL

The town of Springfield was the home of one superstar — actor Brad Pitt was born there as well. Lucas and Brad even attended the same school, Kickapoo High School. After Lucas graduated, he followed in Mr. Pitt's footsteps and moved to L.A. to pursue his career in showbiz. His talent and creativity caught the eyes of producers, and soon he was appearing in commercials and winning small roles in TV shows like *Veronica Mars* and *Boston Legal*. He first met the folks at the Disney Channel when he won the role of Ethan in the Disney movie *Halloweentown III*, and his appearance attracted attention so quickly, that fans almost immediately began putting up Web sites and MySpace profiles singing his praises and asking, "Who's that guy?"

HATS OFF!

When *HSM* was being cast, producers knew that Lucas would be perfect for Ryan. And it was Lucas who came up with Ryan's trademark — his awesome collection of hats. "[The stylist] asked me: 'Do you have anything interesting you want to do with the character?' and I said, 'Hats.' He put one on me . . . and went out and got, like, 50 hats, and I wore one in every single scene."

LUCAS THE SINGER

Unlike his castmates, Lucas isn't planning on releasing a CD of his own, although he did have a blast performing on tour with the *HSM* cast, and admits he does love the thrill of singing live to an audience. "Maybe someday down the line, I'll give it a try, but right now I'm focused on this acting thing," he said to Newsday.com.

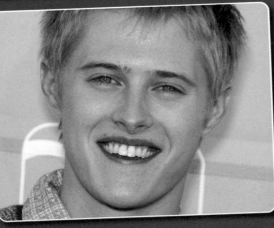

WHAT'S AHEAD

Lucas considers himself lucky to have been a part of the amazing movie franchise. But while you might think Lucas has had his fill of nasty characters, you might be surprised to know that he's looking forward to playing even meaner parts! "I think the villain is always the fun part," he joked to Newsday.com. "I think every actor would love the chance to play the really evil character, the one that the audience boos at. I think that might be something I'd like to try for."

MONIQUE COLEMAN: SHE'S THE DANCING QUEEN!

Bubbly Monique Coleman may seem like she was "tailor-made" to play Taylor McKessie, but the talented 20-something did have a few reservations about returning to high school — especially since she's actually a college grad.

THE ACTING BUG BITES

Monique was bitten by the acting bug at an early age, and she began her career by auditioning for roles in local community theaters. But she didn't make the move to California until she was older. "It was always important to me and my family that I maintained a very normal life, a regular childhood," she explained to *Tiger Beat* magazine. "Even though I knew I wanted to perform . . . I always knew I wanted to complete my education and be prepared for anything. In show business, things don't always work out exactly as you want them to, and you need to have skills to back you up."

TOTALLY TAYLOR

When Monique auditioned for the role of Taylor, the producers were blown away by her energy and enthusiasm, and they knew she'd be perfect to play Gabriella's bouncy and brainy best friend. "I know I have the same kind of spunk they wanted for Taylor," Monique explained to *Tiger Beat*. "She's someone you want to be friends with, someone who's very welcoming and happy about herself and school. I think I had those qualities, and I think I was able to bring my own love of school to the set."

WORK IT

When she was five years old and living with her mom in New York City, a car spun out of control and hit her and her cousin. Monique was in a body cast and had to have a pin put in her leg. After months of physical therapy, Monique was not only able to walk again, but she was soon dancing and performing again. "I learned that it takes hard work to attain something that's precious to you," she told *Tiger Beat*. "But I also learned to never take anything for granted, and to never think. 'Oh, I can't do that.' It may take work to do it, but yes, I believe I can do anything I set my mind to."

MONIQUE'S MOVES

Because of her injury as a child, it was twice as sweet for Monique to strut her stuff on *Dancing with the Stars* a few seasons ago. "I am like the biggest fan of that show," she told Newsday.com. "I've watched it every season, and I'm the biggest fan in the world. When I found out I was going to be on it, I was so thrilled. I've always had a passion for dancing, and this just brought it out in me, completely."

HSM MEMORIES

Although she is sad to see it end, Monique is proud to have been a part of something as special as *High School Musical*, and especially proud that Taylor has become a role model for young women across the world. "*High School Musical* is definitely a responsibility, and one that we stepped up to the plate to meet, especially for me and my character," she told *Tiger Beat*. ". . . I think it's important for girls to see a movie that isn't all about 'the boy' or 'the relationship,' or 'Am I pretty enough?' or 'Am I cute enough?' Here the focus is more on 'Am I talented?' or 'Am I smart?' and I think those are better, more important questions for girls to ask themselves."

ZAC EFRON: "The message from the movie is that you have to be yourself, walk your own path. Don't listen to all the pressures that come from the outside world. Troy starts out as this hotshot stud, but he's been given that name by his peers. Throughout the movies, he changes, he transforms, and he discovers who he is and what he believes in. In each movie, you see him change, and that's great, because it shows people that you don't have to 'live up or down to' your reputation. You just have to be true to you."

VANESSA ANNE HUDGENS: "The movie shows that you can overcome your doubts and fears, and you can become anything you want to be. I think that's why the story is so popular. It goes beyond just the relationship between Troy and Gabriella, and the dancing and singing. It's also got a powerful message about being who you want to be."

ASHLEY TISDALE: "In my own life, I've always believed that you have to work hard to make your dreams come true, and I've also believed you should never, never follow the crowd. The movies show how true that message is, because the people who work hard and follow their dreams are rewarded."

45

CORBIN BLEU: "Working with Kenny Ortega was incredible, because he's a dancer and he's able to make you see and understand things through dance. And of course the character I play is definitely a fun change — I've always played some form of nerd, so playing a jock was great fun. And I think every actor loves the chance to be in a musical."

LUCAS GRABEEL: "Singing actually got me into acting, and once I moved to Los Angeles, I thought I would be just acting, and that I wouldn't be doing much singing anymore. And dancing — wow! I never thought I'd be dancing in a movie. But then *High School Musical* came along — it came out of nowhere, and I don't think anyone thought we'd have this much success."

MONIQUE COLEMAN: "It's amazing to me that so many fans love the movies and watch them over and over. There's something about it that really connects with fans, I think, and they can't get enough of the story. When I meet fans, they always tell me, 'I wish my school was like East High,' and 'I wish I had a friend like Taylor,' so you can see they're really connecting to it."

ZAC EFRON:
BEST ALL-AROUND STUDENT!

"I would flip out if I got a 'B' and not an 'A' in school, but I also have to admit I was a bit of a class clown. If I got along with a teacher and felt comfortable, there was no end to my telling jokes or making people laugh in class. And while there were always cliques in school, I was lucky. I wasn't part of any clique. I had friends all over school."

VANESSA ANNE HUDGENS:
PROM QUEEN WANNABE!

"I know this sounds so stupid, but . . . I was home-schooled, and I missed a lot of the whole high school opportunities. You see high school in the movies, and you imagine that's how it would be, and it looked like fun. I always wanted to be prom queen, that's was a dream of mine. So now it's really exciting to know that I'll be going to a prom — as Gabriella of course, but I'll be there!"

ASHLEY TISDALE:
NEW GIRL IN TOWN

"I'd moved from New Jersey to California, and everyone had grown up together except me. I was quiet and shy, and I was in and out of school doing shows, so I was never in a particular group. I wasn't in drama in school because my drama teacher didn't like me at all. I know what it feels like to not fit in — one of the reasons I hope I'm not mean like Sharpay is because of my own experience with high school. Still, the kids there voted me 'Most Likely To Be An Actress,' so I guess they knew!"

47

CORBIN BLEU: GUY ON STAGE

"I tried to play baseball and basketball in school, because that's what the really popular guys did, and I failed miserably. When I started dancing, the guys would all tell me that was 'girly' and they said I wouldn't be able to get any girls to like me if I couldn't play sports. But they were very misinformed, because when you're involved with theater, you meet tons of girls — so it all worked out for me in the end!"

LUCAS GRABEEL: TEACHER'S PET, EVEN TODAY!

"I just like to go back home and visit my old teachers. They were always very supportive of me. I visited one of my favorite teachers, my fifth-grade art teacher, Sandi Baker, at Logan Rogersville Upper Elementary School, and there was a mob of kids there who wanted autographs. It was fun! Some of my teachers were extra-special to me, and I always want to show my gratitude to them for what they gave me."

MONIQUE COLEMAN: RAH RAH!

"I'm a little like Taylor — she's a leader and she's smart — but I'm not as good in math and science, that's for sure. In my school, I was a cheerleader — which is funny because in *HSM* I hate jocks so much, and I was one!"